MG 4.9/2.0

TIME MACHINE MAGAZINE

Time Machine Magazine books are published by Stone Arch Books
A Capstone Imprint
1710 Roe Crest Drive
North Mankato, Minnesota 56003
www.mycapstone.com

Library of Congress Cataloging-in-Publication Data
Terrell, Brandon, 1978- author.
Harmony and hoops / by Brandon Terrell.
        pages cm. – (Sports Illustrated kids. Time machine magazine)
Summary: After Nate's middle school basketball team suffers a frustrating loss, he
and his cousin Rachel travel back in time to see the 1992 Dream Team in Barcelona,
and learn about teamwork—but he still needs to convince the other players on his
team to share the ball.

ISBN 978-1-4965-2596-3 (library binding)
ISBN 978-1-4965-2705-9 (paperback)
ISBN 978-1-4965-2709-7 (ebook pdf)

1. Olympic Games (25th : 1992 : Barcelona, Spain)—Juvenile fiction. 2. Sports
illustrated—Juvenile fiction. 3. Basketball stories. 4. Teamwork (Sports)—Juvenile
fiction. 5. Time travel—Juvenile fiction. 6. Cousins—Juvenile fiction. 7. Barcelona
(Spain)—History—Juvenile fiction. [1. Olympic Games (25th : 1992 : Barcelona, Spain)—
Fiction. 2. Basketball—Fiction. 3. Teamwork (Sports)—Fiction. 4. Time travel—Fiction. 5.
Cousins—Fiction. 6. African Americans—Fiction. 7. Barcelona (Spain)—Fiction. 8. Spain—
Fiction.] I. Garcia, Eduardo, illustrator. II. Title.
  PZ7.T273Har 2016
  813.6–dc23
  [Fic]
                                          2015035798

Editor: Nate LeBoutillier
Designer: Ted Williams
Illustrator: Eduardo Garcia

Photo Credits: Sports Illustrated: Manny Millan, 124
Design Elements: Shutterstock

*Dream Team: How Michael, Magic, Larry, Charles, and the Greatest Team of All Time
Conquered the World and Changed the Game of Basketball Forever* by Jack McCallum
was used as a reference for some of the elements of chapter four.

Printed in the United States of America in
North Mankato, Minnesota
102015   009221CGS16

TIME MACHINE MAGAZINE

HARMONY AND HOOPS

BY BRANDON TERRELL

STONE ARCH BOOKS
a capstone imprint

"For me, the Dream Team is number one of anything I've done in basketball because there will never be another team like it. There can't be."

—Earvin "Magic" Johnson

CHAPTER 1

Coach Webster's hands formed a T as he shouted, "Time out!"

The referee nearest the coach blew his whistle, sending the sweaty squads jogging to their separate benches. With just one minute remaining, the Wells Warriors Middle School basketball team was down two points to the visiting Prairie Hill Gophers.

Thirteen-year-old Nate Winstead squeezed into the Warriors' team huddle as Coach Webster fired up his players.

"This is the part of the game where real leaders step up," Coach Webster growled. Despite his small size, Coach Webster was a tornado on two feet. "Leaders take control of their own destiny. Got it?"

"Loud and clear, Coach," said Jaden Kershaw, nodding. Jaden, the Warriors' point guard and best player, wiped his close-cropped black hair and forehead with a towel. He seemed to think Coach Webster's pep talk was only directed at him.

The huddle broke, and the players ran back onto the court. Nate resumed his usual position: sitting at the end of the bench next to the water bottles, towels, and other benchwarmers. Nate generally rode the pine more minutes than he played. But he was tall, had a decent jump shot, and was aggressive on defense. All qualities Coach Webster looked for in a Warrior. But Nate had a tough time with taking control, and when he was on the court, his nerves took over. So he sat on the bench where he was less likely to turn the ball over.

"Let's go, Warriors!" a familiar voice shouted. Nate turned for a glimpse of the bleachers behind him. He tracked the source of the cheer through a blue and yellow sea of family and friends to his dad, who gave him an enthusiastic thumbs-up.

Next to his dad stood Nate's cousin, Rachel Young. While she cheered when appropriate, she more often intensely studied the court and players like a general studying a battleground. The two cousins were the same age, but Rachel was naturally athletic and graceful while Nate was, well, not.

The ref blew his whistle. Kendrick Johnson made the inbound pass to Jaden, who called out the play.

"Warrior One!" Jaden commanded.

The play was a basic pick-and-roll. But with Jaden playing point, nothing was ever basic. He dribbled left, where the Warriors' center, Paolo Travini, set a perfect pick on the Gopher defender. Jaden breezed past. He dribbled the ball between his legs as Paolo rolled down the lane toward the hoop.

"Hit me!" Paolo shouted. He lifted his massive hand into the air. He was wide open.

Instead of passing, though, Jaden stopped and put up a jump shot that clanged off the rim. The Gophers' center brought down the rebound.

"Defense!" Coach Webster shouted. He paced the sideline. With his crisp black suit and waddling steps, Coach Webster reminded Nate of that Batman villain, The Penguin.

The Warriors dashed back on D. Nate looked up at the scoreboard on the gymnasium wall. The clock showed just 35 seconds remaining.

The Gophers' point guard tried to kill the clock but found himself trapped. He tried to pass out of the trap, but the ball was knocked away by Victor Gonzalez, the Warriors' shortest and fastest player. Vic snatched the ball, spied an open lane, and took off on a fast break. Andy Hewitt, the Warriors' other forward, broke open on the left side of the court. He had an easy lay-up, but Vic either didn't see him or didn't care. He pulled up and shot a risky three-pointer over a rushing Gophers defender.

Airball.

Nate looked at the clock. Just 23 seconds left.

"Time out!" Coach Webster threw his whiteboard on the floor. It rattled around at his feet.

The Warriors hustled over to the bench.

"What's going on out there?!" Coach Webster hollered. "Smart shots only, for crying out loud. We're not looking for glory here, just a *win*."

"Don't worry," Jaden said, "I'll get open."

"Nah. I got this," Vic added.

"I'll be open in the paint," Paolo said.

"Knock it off," Coach Webster said. "We're not even on offense! We're going to need to foul to get the ball back."

When the Gophers passed the ball inbounds, the first thing Andy Hewitt did was hack the guard who caught the pass.

The ref blew his whistle. "Foul!" He pointed at Andy. "One-and-one. Everyone on the line."

The players began to walk toward the Gophers' basket.

"Winstead!" Coach Webster waved him over. Nate's heart leapt into his throat and tried to crawl out. He stood, stripped off his practice jersey, and walked over to the coach. Coach Webster placed a hand on his shoulder. "You're going in for Hewitt."

"Okay, Coach."

Nate's hands shook. He'd never been in during a high-pressure situation. Usually, he only played when it was a blowout.

"Hewitt," he squeaked. He hoped he didn't sound too scared and held out his hand to high-five Andy as he passed.

But the forward scowled, saying, "What's Coach doing? He can't pull me with ten seconds left."

"I dunno," was all Nate could muster.

Nate took his place on the line between two Gophers as the foul shooter waited for the ball. If the Gophers guard made the first foul shot, he would get a second. If not, the ball was up for grabs. When the ref bounced the ball over, the shooter let out a sharp breath, spun the ball, and dribbled it three times. The second the ball left his hands, the other players began to jostle for position and box one another out under the hoop. Nate was surprised to be hit in the chest with an elbow. The ball hit the rim and then the backboard, rattled around, and missed the mark.

Paolo came up with the rebound. He dished the ball to Vic, who evaded a defender and raced up the court. Nate headed toward the hoop.

"Pass!" Paolo shouted, holding his long arm up.

Vic surged forward. Two Gophers trapped him, leaving Nate wide open.

"Dish the ball to Nate!" Rachel's voice stood out among the mass of cheering fans.

Nate stood under the hoop with absolutely no one around him, terrified that Vic would actually take Rachel's advice.

Ten . . . nine . . . eight. . . . .

"Gimme the ball!" Jaden barked as he cut in front Vic. The ball squirted loose as Vic dribbled to his left to avoid a collision. Jaden gobbled it up.

Five . . . four . . . three . . . .

"Pass! Over here!" Paolo jumped up and down, waving his arms like he was stranded on a deserted island and was signaling a rescue boat.

"Shoot!" Coach Webster shouted.

Jaden pulled up and fired an off-balance jump shot. Every eye in the gymnasium watched as the ball sailed high. Time slowed, stopped. Nate stood in the lane, staring up at it.

Jaden's shot clanged off the rim.

A Gopher was there to secure the rebound, and the buzzer echoed through the gymnasium.

After slapping hands and mumbling congratulations to the Gophers on their victory, Nate and the rest of the Warriors shuffled off toward the locker room with their heads bowed in defeat.

The mood in the locker room was about as foul as the scent. The Warriors dressed in silence. Coach Webster had nothing to say. He seethed and paced, opened his mouth to speak, then thought better. He walked out of the locker room, slamming the door behind him. This left the sullen Warriors alone to bang their lockers closed and shove their sweaty uniforms into duffel bags.

"We could've had that game," Paolo finally muttered as he slammed his locker shut. "I was totally open."

"Yeah," Vic chimed in from the wooden bench in front of his locker. "And so was I. Had a clear lane to the hoop."

"What a joke." Jaden shrugged on his black winter coat. "You all know I'm the only one who's in charge of this team."

Paolo rushed forward and wagged a finger in Jaden's face.

Jaden slapped Paolo's finger away. "Back off," he said.

"Make me." Paolo stood his ground.

The two were eye to eye, nose to nose, clenched fist to clenched fist. The rest of the team slowly surrounded them.

"Stop acting like you're the only ones on this team with any talent," Vic said, stepping into the mix.

Nate could sense that whatever was going to happen, it wasn't going to be good. He moved quickly, gathering the rest of his things in his duffel bag. Then he crammed his blue and yellow Warriors stocking cap onto his head and slunk out the locker room door unseen while the rest of his fractured team fought with one another.

CHAPTER 2

"You guys looked terrible," Rachel said. Her breath plumed in front of her, and she wore a floppy stocking cap. "And that game got ugly at the end."

"Gee, thanks for the pep talk, Coach," Nate said. He cupped his chilly hands and blew into them for warmth.

"I'm surprised your inflated egos and enlarged heads could even run down the court without falling over," Rachel continued. She put up a shot on the old, wooden backboard hanging above the cabin's garage door.

Nothing but net.

Clear Lake was a couple miles outside the town of Wells, where Nate and his parents lived. Rachel and her mom, who had recently moved back to town, were temporarily staying at the cabin with their grandpa.

A thin layer of snow covered the ground, and the lake behind them was icing over as winter began to sneak in and make itself comfortable. Still, the driveway was clear enough for the two teens to practice.

Nate grabbed the ball. "Well, we're gonna need to get our act together if we want to beat Eagleton next game. They're undefeated." His hook shot arced high and struck the siding of the cabin above the hoop.

Just then Rachel's mom, Eve, poked her head out the front door. "Come thaw out," she said. "I've got hot chocolates waiting."

Nate and Rachel hung their coats and hats on the rack inside the front door and walked to the cabin's kitchen. Nate's parents sat on stools around the kitchen island, mugs of coffee in front of them.

"Hey, Grandpa Sam," Nate said as he passed his grandfather, a barrel-chested man who acted gruff but had the heart of a kitten.

"Hey, kiddo."

Seated at the end of the island was a man with a shock of white hair atop his head, a thin face, and bright blue eyes. "Top me off, will ya?" the man asked Grandpa Sam with a smile. He waved his empty coffee mug.

"Hold your horses, Harry," Grandpa Sam replied.

Harry Underhill and Grandpa Sam had once worked at rival magazines in New York City, but were now retired. Harry lived in a cabin on the other side of Clear Lake.

Nate's eyes fluttered over to the hallway, where a set of stairs led to the cabin's basement. The room had a magnetic draw on him. First, it was filled with amazing sports memorabilia from Grandpa Sam's many years as a sports journalist. Things like signed basketballs and boxing gloves and even a baseball mitt once worn by Mickey Mantle.

But it also had a filing cabinet filled with back issues of *Sports Illustrated* that Nate and Rachel had used to travel back in time to witness historic moments. It was something far beyond their understanding, and something they'd never believe if they hadn't experienced it firsthand.

Nate grabbed a mug of hot chocolate and slid into a chair at the table. Rachel did the same. She plunked a bag of mini-marshmallows in front of them, and the two loaded their mugs with them.

"You guys missed a good game yesterday," Nate's dad said to the older men. He was in full brag mode. "The coach called Nate's number at crunch time. But they lost a close one."

"Because their team is filled with ball hogs who don't know how to pass," Rachel added.

"Sounds like you guys need your own version of 'The Greatest Game That Nobody Saw,'" Harry said, taking a swig of coffee.

Nate was confused. "What does that mean?"

Harry smirked. With his comment, he'd cast out a line, and had hooked a big fish. "You remember the Dream Team, right?"

"The 1992 Olympics basketball team with Michael Jordan and Magic Johnson, right?" Rachel asked it like a question, but Nate was pretty sure that was just for show. Rachel was an encyclopedia of sports knowledge.

"*Like Mike*," Nate's dad began to sing. "*If I could be like Mike. I wanna be, I wanna be like—*"

"Dad?"

Nate's dad saw the look of embarrassment on Nate's face and shrugged. "What?" he said. "Michael Jordan was the single greatest basketball player who ever touched a ball. As a kid, my room was a floor-to-ceiling Jordan shrine."

"It certainly was," Grandpa Sam said.

"In fact," Nate's dad continued. "Pretty sure I still have my Air Jordan high tops somewhere."

Nate wondered if his dad thought this made him cooler, because in reality, it was having the opposite effect. Especially the singing part.

Harry went back to telling his story. He ticked off names on his fingers. "Larry Bird. Patrick Ewing. Charles Barkley. Karl Malone. It was the greatest team of players ever assembled."

Grandpa Sam took the bounce pass from Harry and said, "Up until the '92 Summer Games, professional athletes couldn't compete in the Olympics. Now these guys were used to playing against each other, not beside one another."

Harry took over the story again. "Before the games began in Barcelona, the team went to Monte Carlo for some practice and team-building. They played a few exhibition games, amd they thoroughly enjoyed the casinos and the night life. Michael Jordan and Chuck Daly, the team's coach, played golf every day."

"Really roughing it," Nate's dad chimed in.

"The day after they played an exhibition game against France," Grandpa Sam said, "Daly split the groups into two teams—Team Jordan versus Team Magic—and they scrimmaged."

"Very few people were there to see it," Harry concluded. "To this day, Jordan says it was the best game of basketball he ever played."

"Cool," Rachel said.

"They came out of Monte Carlo as a team, and averaged 117 points a game in the Olympics," Harry said. "And yours truly scored the first exclusive interview with Coach Chuck Daly after the Games. A cover story and everything."

"Yeah, yeah." Grandpa Sam waved him off dismissively. "So you've been reminding me for over twenty years."

"Where were you, Grandpa?" Nate asked.

He pointed at Nate's dad and Rachel's mom. "I took time off from work that summer, and we went on a family vacation. Don't regret it a bit."

Nate and Rachel slurped down their hot chocolates. When their bellies were warm and their fingers had regained feeling, Rachel turned to Nate and said, "Wanna play PIG?"

"You're on."

"And I should really be going," Harry said, standing. "Three cups is my limit. In fact, I need to make a pit stop before I go."

"You know where the bathroom is," Grandpa Sam said.

Nate and Rachel suited up in their winter gear and headed back outside. The wind had picked up. It nipped at Nate's cheeks and nose and made his eyes water.

"I'll start you off easy," Rachel said, sinking a jump shot from ten feet away. She fired a crisp chestpass over to Nate.

He put up a shot from the same place, and it bounced off the front of the rim.

"*P*!" Rachel shouted. "Man, this is gonna be a quick game."

She snatched up the ball, dribbled it past the three-point range, and put up her next shot. It bounced high off the rim, flirted with the top of the backboard, but came down through the hoop.

"Count it!" she boasted.

"No way!" Nate jogged over to retrieve the ball. As he did, however, his foot caught a patch of ice in the driveway. He slipped, tried to regain his balance, but couldn't hold on.

He fell face first into a dirty, shallow pile of snow.

As Nate pulled himself from the freezing pile of muck, he could hear Rachel trying to stifle laughter.

"Funny," he said, spitting snow and grit onto the driveway. "Real funny."

While Rachel stayed outside, Nate went back in to clean himself off. He ditched his coat on a rack by the door and beelined past the kitchen, too embarrassed to explain to his parents and Grandpa Sam what had happened to his face and hands.

Nate snagged a towel off a hook by the sink in the bathroom and quickly wiped the dirty snow off of himself. He looked in the mirror to make sure he'd done a decent job and muttered to himself before rehanging the towel. As he passed the stairs leading to the basement, he noticed a light was on.

"Weird," he said, deciding to check it out.

Harry stood in the middle of the basement, next to a glass case containing Grandpa Sam's collection of baseball bobbleheads. He had a smile on his face as he studied his surroundings.

When Harry looked up and saw Nate, he jerked back, startled.

"Sorry," Nate said.

"Quite all right," Harry said. "You know, your grandpa is a smart man. Keeping all these treasures."

"Yeah," Nate agreed. "I love this room." He paused, then asked, "Do you have a bunch of stuff at your place?"

Harry shook his head.

"Why not?"

"Well, your grandpa had Ruth and the kids to come home to. A place to settle down. Me, I've always been a solo act. I traveled the world, saw amazing sights, and ate exotic foods. My passport is the only collectible I ever needed." He picked up a magazine propped on a shelf beside an old, autographed basketball. "Still, this place is pretty magical."

"Yeah," Nate said. "It is." *If you only knew*, he thought.

Harry flipped through the magazine in his hands before passing it over to Nate. "Here," he said. "In case you're curious to read more about the Dream Team."

He slipped his hands in his pockets and wandered back toward the stairs, peering at each shelf and case as he went. Then he walked up the steps and out of sight.

Nate glanced down at the magazine Harry had handed him. It was an issue of *Sports Illustrated*

from February of 1991. On the cover, five amazing basketball players grinned out at him. Michael Jordan and Magic Johnson sat in front, shoulder-to-shoulder, their arms folded. Behind them stood Charles Barkley, Patrick Ewing, and Karl Malone.

A red banner across the top read: Dream Team.

"'Watch out, world!'" Nate read aloud from the text at the bottom of the cover. "'This could be America's 1992 Olympic five.'"

A blue spark danced on his fingertips, there and then gone. A normal person would have dropped the magazine, screamed, and stomped on it as if it was on fire. Nate, though, knew what the spark meant. When he flipped open the magazine, a second, larger crackle of energy wrapped around his right hand.

"I gotta show Rachel," he said.

Nate tucked the *Sports Illustrated* under his shirt. Before he left the basement, he glanced up at the shelf to the spot where Harry had found the magazine. Next to the autographed ball, Nate spied two slips of paper. A trace of blue energy suddenly shot out from beneath his shirt, coursed its way through the air, and flitted over the slips of paper.

"Whoa!" Puzzled, Nate stepped over and pulled the slips of paper from the shelf.

They were tickets, two of them. Each read: *Gold Medal Basketball. 1992. Barcelona*. The Olympic rings decorated the tickets.

Nate realized that Grandpa Sam had a set of unused tickets from the game. He never used them because he went on vacation instead of going to Barcelona to cover the Olympics.

Without hesitation, Nate withdrew the magazine and stuck the tickets into its back pages. Then he made sure the *SI* was once again safe under his shirt and raced back up the steps. As he reached the kitchen, where the adults were still sipping coffee and Harry was saying his goodbyes, Nate's dad suddenly called out, "Whoa! Hold on, LeBron."

Nate came to a stuttering stop. Beneath his shirt, he felt the blue energy tickle his chest and stomach. He hoped his shirt's fabric hid the glow.

"What?" Nate pressed a hand to his chest. Goosebumps spread quickly across his arms and back.

His dad eyed him up suspiciously. "Everything okay?" he asked.

"Yeah," Nate said, stepping lightly from one foot to the other. "I just . . . I'm amped up to beat Rachel at PIG is all."

His dad chewed on his bottom lip, his eyes still locked on Nate.

The strongest blast of energy yet snaked from the magazine. It zapped Nate right in the belly button, tickling him. He doubled over in a fit that was half-coughing and half-laughing. Then, before his dad could ask anything else, Nate broke for the front door.

"Five minutes!" his dad called after him.

"Okay," Nate managed to say.

As he grabbed his coat and shoved open the front door with his shoulder, Nate heard his dad say, "How many marshmallows did that kid eat?"

Rachel was sinking a free throw from a smudged line she'd toed in the driveway snow when Nate burst outside. "Check it out!" he shouted, fumbling in his coat to withdraw the *Sports Illustrated*. He stumbled, nearly biffing it in the snow again.

He held out the magazine as another surge of energy escaped the its pages.

Rachel didn't even have to look at the cover. "We're going to the 1992 Summer Games!" she said, zipping up her coat and dropping her basketball in the snow.

"Yup," said Nate. He glanced back at the cabin, just to make sure that no one was watching them out the window or anything. The coast was clear.

He and Rachel huddled around each other, their breath puffing out in front of them, swirling together and dissipating in the cold afternoon air.

Nate's fingers were going numb, making it difficult to flip open the *Sports Illustrated*. He fumbled with it a bit before finding the article he was looking for. It was entitled "Lords of the

Rings," written by Jack McCallum. Nate began to read.

"*It's a red, white, and blue dream,*" he said. The cobalt energy intensified until the air around Nate and Rachel was charged. Electricity surrounded them. Nate continued. "*The five players who grace this week's cover, playing together, determined to restore America's lost basketball dignity, in the 1992 Olympic Games in Barcelona. What's the chance of this dream coming true? Not bad. Not bad at all.*"

"Here we go," Rachel said, pulling her stocking cap down. "Hold on to your hat."

The world around Nate and Rachel shifted and spun. It became hazy and out of focus, like they were standing in the eye of a storm.

Three brilliant flashes of light erupted from the magazine, and tendrils of energy snaked around them.

And then, in an instant, everything went black.

CHAPTER 3

The darkness turned to light.

Hot, blinding light.

Nate staggered back and shielded his eyes. It was like he and Rachel had traveled to the surface of the sun. He stumbled, fell backward, and landed hard in what felt like lava. Around him, he heard kids laughing, people talking, and waves crashing against rocks.

"Nate? Where are you?" He heard Rachel calling out to him, though he refused to open his eyes to look for her.

"I'm . . . I'm here. Wherever here is."

Slowly, Nate peeled open one eyelid. His vision adjusted to the light, and he began to see things. Water stretching to the horizon. A beach filled with umbrellas and people in bathing suits laying on towels and basking in the warmth of the sun.

"We're . . . we're on a beach," he said, stunned.

"A beach? No way!"

Rachel was beside him, though she still had one hand plastered over both eyes. She removed it, squinting against the sun but taking in her surroundings.

They were, in fact, on a beach made of beautiful white sand. Towering palm trees swayed high above them in the gentle, salty breeze. The water was as blue as Nate had ever seen before.

"Little different than subzero temps," Rachel said.

Nate's eyes caught sight of all the beachgoers in their swimwear and said, "Yep. Just a little different." He still had the Dream Team *Sports Illustrated* in his bare hand. It was odd, but his hands and fingers were still cold. His whole body was, actually. As the sweltering temperature began to thaw him out, his nose and ears turned beet red, and his fingers and toes began to tingle.

Nate looked down at what he was wearing. Instead of a winter coat and stocking cap, he now had on a brightly colored T-shirt and cargo shorts, along with a pair of flip-flops. Rachel wore a hot pink tank top and khaki shorts.

Rachel laughed. "Ha! Nice fanny pack, dude!" She nodded at Nate's waist, where a black and neon green pouch was strapped across like a belt.

Nate groaned. "Is this what people wore in the 90s?" he asked.

"Look around you. It gets way worse."

Oh man, she's right, Nate thought, as he noticed the array of colors and fashions. Neon and pastel colored clothes, pinned jeans and frayed, denim shorts. Men and women alike had poofy hair that made it look like hair stylists in the 90s were trying to make everyone look like poodles.

Nate shook his head in amazement. Then he unzipped his pack and discovered it was filled with money—both paper and coins, though Nate couldn't tell how much the odd-looking currency was worth in American dollars—and assorted maps of Europe, Spain, and the city of Barcelona.

Well, that's a relief, he thought. At least they could pay for food and maybe a place to stay while they were there.

Then, a jolt of fear struck Nate. He quickly flipped through the pages of the *Sports Illustrated*.

"What are you doing?" Rachel asked.

"Looking for . . . *aha!*" Relief washed over him. He plucked the tickets from the magazine's back pages and showed them to Rachel.

"They were on the shelf in Grandpa Sam's basement," he explained. "Next to the *Sports Illustrated.*"

"And now they're ours," Rachel said. "Nice work."

Nate secured them in his fanny pack.

"So is this Barcelona?" Rachel looked around at the beach.

Nate had no idea why, but for some reason, he suspected they weren't in Barcelona. In the distance, he saw a promenade filled with shops and restaurants. A crowd of people in bathing suits strolled along it.

On many of the signs, Nate could make out the words: Monte Carlo.

"We're not in Barcelona," he said. "We're in Monte Carlo."

"We are?" Rachel looked confused. "Where's that?"

Nate got out his map and unfolded it, knowing full well he looked like a tourist. He slid his finger up the coast of Spain and through France until he got to the principality of Monaco. "Here," he said, pointing at Monaco. Monte Carlo was right next to the blue of the Mediterranean Sea.

"But why are we here when the Games are in Barcelona?" Rachel asked.

As if to answer her question, a tall man with striking black hair and a thin mustache stopped beside them. "*Excuse moi*," he said in French, followed by broken English. "Are you looking for . . . basketball exhibition game?"

Nate nodded. It was all clicking into place. "The Dream Team?" he asked.

The man nodded. "*Oui.* They are playing against the French national team this evening. Stade Louis II Arena."

"Yes," Nate said. "We're going to the game."

The man offered directions to the arena before continuing on his way.

"Wait," Rachel said as they began to walk through the glittering, tourist-filled city. "If the

Dream Team is in Monte Carlo, then the Summer Games haven't started yet."

Nate nodded. "Remember, they spent a week here before the opening ceremony in Barcelona. And if they're playing France tonight, then tomorrow morning the team will face off against one another and play The Greatest Game. You know, the one that Harry told us about." He sped up his pace. "Come on, let's check it out."

Stade Louis II Arena was easy to find. All they had to do was follow the massive throngs of people who all headed to the same place. The arena was an enormous structure. Palm trees and shrubs lined the street outside the main entrance, where nine stone arches rose side by side into the air. The street outside the arena was jam-packed. Many people wore U.S.A. shirts or shirts featuring players from the team. A young boy in a Magic Johnson T-shirt bounced a basketball through the crowd.

A sign over the outdoor ticket booth said *Sold Out* in both English and French.

"Dang it!" Nate's shoulders sagged in defeat. "I should have guessed."

Rachel, however, was not fazed. "Hold on a second," she said.

An older man with deep creases in his face stood under the shade of a palm tree. A sign rested against the tree trunk. It said, *Tix 4 Sale*. From a distance, Nate watched as Rachel approached and spoke to the man. He nodded and produced a pair of tickets.

Rachel waved Nate over. "Unzip that fanny pack, dude," she said.

Nate paid for the tickets with what he thought was the right amount of money. The man kept saying, "Francs. Francs." When the man was happy, and they walked off with a pair of tickets to the game, Nate and Rachel had used up a fair amount of their cash. It made Nate nervous, not knowing how long they'd be in the past and how much money they'd need.

Still, they had to see the exhibition game somehow.

Stade Louis II arena was abuzz with activity as Nate and Rachel found their seats. Nate noticed that despite the grand size of the venue, the packed gymnasium didn't hold as many fans as regular pro arenas. The gym at Nate's high school held about 2,000 people. There were maybe twice that many fans at Stade Louis II. When the NBA all-stars took the court to warm up, the place erupted. The fans made themselves known with thunderous applause and whistling. Camera flashes popped like lightning bugs across the stands.

"I can't believe it's really them," Nate said.

Rachel was too starstruck to respond.

From Nate's vantage point, they were just small figures jogging onto the court. But even so, the professional basketball players appeared larger than life. Having a sportswriter for a grandpa helped the kids identify the legends. Michael Jordan. Magic Johnson. Larry Bird and Charles Barkley.

"There's Karl Malone!" Rachel shouted, pointing. "And John Stockton!"

"Patrick Ewing. Scottie Pippen."

"Chris Mullin, Clyde Drexler, David Robinson."

"Don't forget Christian Laettner."

They were led by Chuck Daly, a gruff-looking man in a suit with a thick head of hair and menacing eyebrows. Coach Daly stood alongside the bench, hands on hips, watching the players.

The French team looked to be about as big of fans as the spectators. Nate was surprised to see some of them even had cameras on the bench, snapping shots of the American athletes.

When the game began, Team USA looked so . . . well, average. Nate wished there was a better word for it. They were completely out of sync, allowing France the early lead. The crowd, including a man Nate overheard someone call Prince Rainier, watched on in amazement. Despite their uneven performance, the men on the U.S. squad were still celebrities. The crowd of fans even began to chant, "*Mah-jique! Mah-jique!*" Magic Johnson waved in recognition.

Toward the end of the first half, something clicked. Whether it was something Coach Daly barked at them, or whether they just finally found their footing, the U.S. team delivered the type of basketball the people of Monte Carlo paid to see.

When the final buzzer sounded, the score was 111-71—not even close. Jordan, Johnson, and the U.S. all-stars had easily handled the French team.

As Nate and Rachel followed the flock of spectators out of the arena, Nate spied Magic Johnson climbing up into the stands to Prince Rainier's personal box to take photos. The prince's grin was visible even from Nate's view on the far side of the court.

Nate and Rachel slipped back with the crowd onto the streets of Monte Carlo. Buzzing with energy from what and who they saw, they had forgotten one very crucial thing.

"So . . . " Rachel said, looking around at the city, "um, now where do we go?"

CHAPTER 4

Rachel's question was simple but important.

Where do we go?

It was late in the evening, and even though the sun had been swallowed by the horizon, it was still humid and hot. Nate was sweating just standing in place.

Monte Carlo was a spectacle of lights. Casinos and hotels and restaurants glowed brightly. Nate had gotten so swept up in the excitement of the basketball exhibition game that he hadn't even thought about where they'd spend the night.

"There's no way the money we have left is going to pay for a hotel room in this city," he said, looking around at the opulent buildings surrounding them.

Rachel agreed.

That left them with no option other than to wander aimlessly through the tourist-laden streets. They walked without a purpose, taking in the sights and marveling about the basketball game they'd just been fortunate enough to witness.

"I mean, my dad took me to a few Celtics game back when I was younger," Rachel said. "But he'd flip out if he knew I just saw Larry Bird in person."

Bird, one of the older players on the team, had injured his back. In order to let it heal, he'd limited his playing time during the exhibition, opting instead to lay on the floor, on his stomach, near the bench.

Rachel rarely spoke of her dad. In fact, Nate couldn't remember a time since she and her mom moved back to Wells that his name had come up. He let it slide, though, instead of asking her more about him.

Finally, they passed a small diner with a sign in the window that said, *All-Nite*.

It was after midnight, but the restaurant still had many customers. The place had been designed to look like a diner out of 1950s America. Red plastic booths lined the walls. Posters of Marilyn Monroe and James Dean hung everywhere. The legs of a large Elvis Presley clock swayed back and forth.

They found an empty booth near the back. It wasn't until Nate sat in the plush, cracked seat that he realized how tired he was and how much his feet hurt. It had been a long day.

"Menus?" The waitress, a young girl with a beehive of hair held together by hairspray and hope, stood at their booth. Before they could answer, she dropped two menus onto the table with a slap.

"Coffee," Rachel said. "Like, a pot of it."

Nate hated coffee, so he opted for a Coca-Cola. The waitress didn't seem to care that they were young or that it was after midnight. So she walked off to get their order without another word.

When their drinks arrived, Rachel filled her mug from the pot and poured an insane amount of sugar and cream into it. They ordered a couple burgers—trying to get a taste of home while they were off traipsing through time—but they weren't nearly as good as Grandpa Sam's grilled burgers.

They sat in the booth for the remainder of the night, much to the irritation of their waitress. She kept giving them the stink-eye, but said nothing. *Probably doesn't want to kick two possibly homeless kids out onto the street*, Nate thought. They watched people come and go. Some were bleary-eyed and ready for bed, Others were still excited over the possibilities a city like Monte Carlo offered in the wee hours of the morning. Once, a man and woman came in, bragging in thick French accents that they had just seen Charles Barkley outside their hotel.

Sometime around four o' clock in the morning, Nate's eyes slipped closed. His shoulders sagged. He began to drift off to the wonderful, much-needed Dreamworld. *Just gonna rest my eyes for a minute or—*

"Nate!" Rachel kicked him in the shin, hard, under the table.

His eyes shot open. "Wha . . . ?!"

"You were falling asleep," she said.

"So? I really wanna." He fully heard the whine in his voice.

Rachel was still buzzed from her pot of coffee. "We can't. Not yet. The sun will be up soon."

He drained the rest of his soda, his third refill, and shook the tiredness away as best he could.

Finally, the city outside the diner began to lighten. Seeing the sun rise was enough to bolster Nate's spirits. He and Rachel paid their bill, leaving what Nate hoped was a hefty tip for their patient waitress, and stepped back out onto the sidewalk.

Even though it was early morning, the temperature was starting to climb. It was going to be another hot day in Monte Carlo.

They made their way back over to Stade Louis II arena. It had been less than twelve hours since the Dream Team had played the French national team, but they were already at the gym for practice.

The scrimmage that many talked about but few had ever seen was about to begin. Nate didn't want to miss it.

They walked the perimeter of the arena, searching for a way inside. As they rounded the building, Nate saw a small door near a set of Dumpsters. It had been propped open.

"There!" He snuck up to the door, hiding behind a Dumpster. Rachel opted to duck behind the trunk of a palm tree, a smarter, less stinky option.

They watched the door for several minutes, waiting for someone to exit, or for someone to close it. Neither happened.

Rachel couldn't wait any longer. "Come on," she whispered, racing through the door.

Nate followed.

The night before, the arena had been packed with people and noise and activity. Now, it was quiet. The calm was unsettling, and Nate felt odd walking through its corridors.

It was humid inside the arena. Before long, Nate was wiping sweat from his forehead with the bottom of his shirt. In the distance, he heard the faint sound of dribbling basketballs. They stole up to a door, peered inside . . .

. . . and there they were, the Dream Team, back on the court, warming up for practice.

Nate and Rachel ducked low and slipped into the gymnasium.

Rows of empty yellow seats lined the gymnasium, a splash of color against the tan hardwood court. Nate opened his mouth to whisper something, but Rachel placed a finger to her lips to silence him. She pointed to their right. Standing there amidst the seats was a lone man with a tripod and a video camera. The camera was trained on the floor, where the players had split into two teams. One team wore navy blue Team USA jerseys; the other, white jerseys.

Coach Daly, wearing a blue polo shirt, said to his team, "All you got now. All you got."

The two teams took their positions. A referee was on hand to help out; he held the ball at center court as David Robinson and Patrick Ewing faced off.

"I can't believe we're here to see this," Nate whispered.

The ref threw the ball into the air, and the game was on!

Robinson swatted it back, where the team's only college kid, Christian Laettner, scooped it up and dished it ahead to Charles Barkley. Barkley dribbled between Michael Jordan and Larry Bird. As he went up for the shot, the Bulls' superstar swatted at Barkley's wrist, drawing the foul.

The shot went in.

"Shoot the fouls!" Daly ordered from the sideline.

Jordan toweled off his bald head as Barkley drained the free throw.

The game was a brawling battle. The younger Jordan faced off against Magic Johnson, who had reigned supreme in the NBA for over a decade. As team captain, Magic called orders.

"Let's go, Blue Team!" he shouted, his words echoing off the empty gym's walls.

The two teams raced up and down the court, trash-talking and jawing at one another. Every time Magic's team would make an amazing play, Jordan's would counter it. The score, however, began to fall toward Magic's team.

That was when Jordan stepped it up.

He took over the game, hitting a jump shot before Magic could cover him. The next time down the court, he passed the ball to Karl Malone, who drained a shot over Barkley.

"Right back at ya!" Jordan yelled to Magic as he jogged back on defense.

Magic came back down the court, passing to David Robinson, who drew a foul on Patrick Ewing.

"All day long!" Magic hollered as they lined up for free throws.

Nate could see the emotions brewing in Jordan's eyes. With Magic's team ahead by five, the White Team fought hard to come back. The competitiveness in each and every one of the all-stars was clear in the way they played.

They watched as Laettner made a set of free throws. As Karl Malone sank a jumper. As Scottie Pippen hit nothing but net.

By the time Jordan lined up and sank the final two free throws, sealing the victory for his White

Team, tensions between he and Magic had risen to almost epic levels. But both teams had played well.

It was the perfect illustration of what Nate imagined a basketball game to be.

Magic draped a towel over his head as Jordan began to sing. "*Sometimes I dream . . . If I could be like Mike . . .*" It was the same commercial jingle Nate's dad had sung.

Before he knew it, a small laugh escaped Nate's lips. He clapped a hand over his mouth.

"Hello?" The cameraman standing nearby had heard the laugh. He craned his neck left and right, searching for the source.

Rachel punched Nate lightly on the shoulder. "Nice going," she whispered. She snuck a look over the seats, grabbed Nate's shirt, and hissed, "Let's go!"

The two teens dashed back out of the gymnasium, down the hall, and out the open door. They burst into the glaring sunlight, their feet slapping the sidewalk, putting the arena and the Dream Team at their backs.

When they finally came to a jog, then a stop, Nate bent over and placed his hands on his knees. He sucked in air, trying to catch his breath. Rachel was not affected.

She looked back in the direction of the arena. "I guess you can call that 'The Greatest Game That *Almost* Nobody Saw," she joked, and the two teens bumped fists.

CHAPTER 5

Having seen Dream Team's exhibition game, as well as their historic—and private—scrimmage against each other, Nate and Rachel decided it was time to head to Barcelona. They used a portion of their remaining money to buy two train tickets. With a whistle and a chug, they rattled down the track, out of Monte Carlo and down the shoreline of the Mediterranean Sea.

After all, the 1992 Summer Games were waiting for them in Spain.

The train ride from Monte Carlo to Barcelona took a little over eight hours, and it was eight hours of the most beautiful scenery Nate had ever seen. At least, what he caught in the rare moments he wasn't sleeping with his mouth open and his head pressed against the window glass.

He woke as the train finally hissed into the Barcelona station.

Beside him, Rachel had also crashed. He nudged her in the side, and her eyes fluttered open.

"That was quick," she said, wiping drool from the side of her mouth.

"We've been asleep about eight hours," he said.

"We have? Crazy."

The two sleepy teens stood and filed out of the train with the other passengers. They made their way through the crowded depot, a glass structure known as the Barcelona Sants. Around them, billboards proudly displayed images of the Olympic rings, and gift shops sold small flags from every country of the world. It felt strange to Nate, watching the rest of the people in the depot with their backpacks and briefcases and luggage. All he had was the silly fanny pack latched onto his—

"Oh no!" Nate shouted. He clutched at his waist. "My fanny pack! I took it off in my seat to get comfortable!"

"Now there's something I never thought I'd hear you say," Rachel joked.

"Knock it off." Nate ran back toward the train. "The gold-medal tickets and the *Sports Illustrated* is inside there."

"Go!" Rachel gave him a shove. "Get back to the train!"

Nate dodged left and right, racing around people and their oversized luggage and strollers. Rachel was at his heels. He was just about back to the train when a voice behind him said, "Young man? Is this yours?"

An older gentleman in a charcoal gray suit stood on the platform. He held the neon pack out in front of him.

Nate sighed. "Oh man," he said. "Thanks. You're a life—"

And he stopped, because he'd finally looked at the man, and the English language had suddenly become the most complicated thing in the world.

The man holding his pack was Harry Underhill.

Harry was younger, of course, and the wrinkles that lined his face the last time Nate saw him were not there yet. His hair was still the same shock of silver, though, which made Nate wonder if it had been that color his whole life.

Harry squinted and waved a hand in front of Nate's face. "Are you okay?" he asked.

Rachel kicked Nate from behind, and Nate was finally able to say, "—saver." He shook his head. "Lifesaver. Sorry. Yes, I'm fine."

"Are you sure?" Harry was amused by Nate's lack of verbal understanding.

"He's just really happy to have his fanny pack again," Rachel said. "He loves that thing." It was clear she knew who they were talking to, but those sorts of things didn't seem to affect her the same way they affected Nate.

"Well then, here you are. Glad I could help." Harry passed off the pack to Rachel, wished them a pleasant day, and hustled off into the busy depot.

Rachel shoved the pack into Nate's stomach. "Come on, Captain Subtle," she said.

Barcelona was a dazzling city with a rich history. Magnificent cathedrals and Gothic castles were nestled among more modern stone buildings. Color and life surprised him at every turn.

The blue skies above were dappled with clouds and a hint of orange. It was nearly dinnertime. The two teens would soon face the same challenge they had in Monte Carlo: They had no where to sleep.

Many signs featured the Olympic rings on flags and posters and banners. Above most was another image that appeared as if created by a paintbrush. A blue dot with an upturned, curved orange mark below it. Below that was a thick red stroke. Together, they created a leaping figure above the rings.

As Nate and Rachel walked along, heads upturned like the tourists they were, a helicopter buzzed overhead. Nate craned his neck to see it just as a trio of teenage boys raced down the block toward them.

"*Ciudado!*" one of the boys shouted. "Watch out!"

The first boy dodged Nate, but clipped Rachel on the side.

"Oof!" she exhaled as she reeled back and fell to the cement.

The three boys came to a screeching stop. One of them, a tall teen with black hair, piercing green eyes, and a long, hooked nose, knelt down. He had a basketball tucked under one arm. "Are you all right?" he asked Rachel in a thick accent. Then he passed the ball off to his buddy, a short kid with a face speckled by pimples, and helped Rachel to her feet.

"*Lo siento*," the boy said. "Carlos is not the most graceful."

Carlos, the boy who'd knocked Rachel over, shyly said, "*Lo siento.*"

Rachel brushed herself off. "S'okay," she said.

"You are American." The dark-haired boy's question didn't come off as one.

"Yeah," Nate said. "Is it that obvious?" He gestured at the obnoxious clothes he was wearing, specifically the vibrant pack at his waist.

The boy smiled. "Ah. Yes." He pointed a thumb at his own shirt, which Nate just then noticed featured a caricature of Charles Barkley. "Go Dream Team," he said.

"Go Dream Team," Nate said.

"I am Alejandro," the hook-nosed teen said.

"Nate. My cousin Rachel."

"Do you play?" Alejandro held out a hand, and the pimple-faced kid passed him back the ball.

Nate nodded. "You bet," he said.

"Both?" He looked at Rachel.

"I dribble circles around him," Rachel said.

Alejandro smiled. "Come then." He began to run down the sidewalk again. Carlos and the short, pimpled friend jogged after him. "*Vamos! Vamos,* Nate and Rachel!"

Nate looked over at Rachel, who gave him a shrug. "Why not?" she asked.

They took off after the trio of locals.

Together, they ran down the sidewalk, first one block, then a second, a third. They cut across a parking lot, and on the far side, Nate saw a high chain-link fence surrounding a stone building. A school, he guessed. Two hoops stood at either end of a cement basketball court, and white lines were roughly painted across the cracked concrete.

Several kids about Nate and Rachel's age were already shooting hoops. Alejandro led them through a narrow gap in the fence.

"*Hola!*" One of the kids slapped high-five to Alejandro and his friends as they joined the group. Nate could feel all eyes on Rachel and him, two outsiders joining the usual crew.

Alejandro huddled together with a few of the others. They spoke in rapid-fire Spanish. Nate had zero clue what they were talking about.

Finally, the huddle broke, and Alejandro jogged over. "Ready to play?" he asked.

Nate nodded. "*Sí.* I mean, sure."

Alejandro laughed. "You are with me, Carlos, and Santiago." The pimpled kid waved as he and the quiet Carlos joined them near the top of the key.

Five other teens—three boys and two girls—joined them. A rail-thin boy Alejandro called Manny stood toe to toe with Alejandro.

"You ready?" Manny asked in clipped English.

He tossed Alejandro the ball.

Nate jogged down the left side of the court, Rachel the right. There were no fans, no set plays or refs calling fouls. Just a bunch of kids running around, tossing a ball, having fun. He'd kind of forgotten what it felt like to actually have fun while playing basketball.

Alejandro dribbled right, using a pick set by Santiago. Nate's defender rushed up to stop Alejandro, leaving Nate open.

Alejandro saw him and fed him the ball. Nate was so surprised that someone was actually passing the ball to him that the ball bounced right

off his chest. "Oof!" Nate said, stepping back as Alejandro scooped up the ball.

"You okay?" he asked Nate.

Nate nodded.

"Then let's try this again." Alejandro dished the ball to Nate, who was ready this time. He put up a bank shot that dropped in.

"*Excellente!*" said Alejandro, pumping his fist.

Rachel jogged over, gave Nate a shove, and said, "Nice shot, dude."

Nate hustled back on defense with the rest of his team, beaming from ear to ear.

CHAPTER 6

They played until the sun disappeared and the sky above was ablaze with streaks of oranges and reds and yellows. Alejandro was a skilled player who had a knack for slipping impossible passes through defenders. He and Rachel connected numerous times on give-and-go plays, to the frustration of the opposing team. If he'd tried out for the Warriors' point guard position, he would have given Jaden Kershaw a run for his money.

When it was too dark to continue, the group said their goodbyes and split off. They slapped high-fives and joked about Alejandro bringing in a pair of "American Dream Teamers" to play.

Nate and Rachel leaned against the chain-link fence to catch their breath. Alejandro came over. "Are you hungry?" he asked.

As if on cue, Nate's stomach rumbled.

"Come." Alejandro draped an arm over Nate's shoulder. "*Mi madre* makes much wonderful food. You will love it."

They walked the streets of Barcelona, which were still crackling with their own energy and buzz. The Opening Ceremony was still a couple of days off, but athletes from around the globe had already arrived. The sound of helicopters in the sky was constant.

Alejandro cut down a narrow alleyway between two brick buildings with metal fire escapes. As they came out onto the next block, the teen pointed to what Nate thought was south or southwest. The glow of lights was more intense than the rest of the city, where a long structure loomed on the horizon. "Over on the hill," he said. "Very near. The *Estadi Olímpic de Montjuïc*. The Olympic stadium. They have been working very hard to prepare it."

Nate had just a moment to marvel at the enormous structure before Alejandro led them through the front door of a stone building. It was an apartment complex. A rickety elevator took them to the fifth floor, where Alejandro walked to the end of the hall.

Nate caught wind of the delicious odors wafting from Alejandro's apartment before they'd even cracked open the door. His stomach rolled and grumbled again. "Easy, boy," he muttered.

The apartment was small but rich in color and life. In the living room, an embroidered quilt with vibrant tones hung above the couch. Portraits and landscape paintings filled the walls. And in every corner sprung potted plants.

"*Hola!*" a voice sang from the unseen kitchen.

Alejandro's mother stepped out to greet her son. She was beautiful, with long, dark hair speckled with white and swept up into a bun. She wore an apron, and was drying her hands with it.

When she saw Nate and Rachel standing in her living room, she was taken aback. Her smile never wavered, though.

"Who are your friends?" she asked.

Alejandro introduced them. "They are visiting from America."

And from the future, thought Nate. *Can't forget that*.

"Well, I am Carmen Vargas," Alejandro's mom said. "Welcome to my home. There is plenty to eat, so please sit."

"See?" Alejandro nudged Nate in the ribs. "Just as I told you."

Nate and Rachel found spots around a circular, chipped wooden table. Alejandro helped his mother bring dishes and silverware and heaping platters of beef empanadas, rice, and beans to the table.

Nate couldn't wait to dive in. The food was beyond delicious. He devoured empanadas until his plate was empty and his stomach was full.

He sat back in his chair. "That. Was. Amazing," he said.

"*Gracias*, Señorita Vargas," Rachel said after swallowing her last bite.

"You are both welcome," Señorita Vargas said.

Nate and Rachel insisted on helping with the dishes. As they carried the empty plates to the kitchen sink, Alejandro asked, "So where are you staying while you are in Barcelona?"

Nate looked at his cousin, who shrugged. "We . . . well, we don't know yet."

Señorita Vargas stopped in her tracks. "You don't? Where is your family?"

"Uh, in America. We're on our own."

"Then you will stay here," Señorita Vargas said matter-of-factly.

"Oh, we can't burden you," Rachel said.

"It is no burden. It is just Alejandro and I. There is a spare room and bed. It is not large, but it is yours."

A weight that Nate didn't realize had been strapped to his back lifted, and he smiled. "*Gracias*," he said.

Señorita Vargas had not been kidding. The bed was a pull-out, the mattress lumpy and misshapen. And they'd had to share it, with Rachel snoring and kicking Nate in her sleep. But even so, it was one of the best nights of sleep Nate had ever had.

The following morning, Alejandro took Nate and Rachel to an outdoor shopping district, where the two Americans used most of the money left in Nate's fanny pack to buy new clothes. Nate even purchased a hand-woven shoulder bag where he could hide the *Sports Illustrated* and the tickets to the gold-medal game.

"Good riddance," he said, dropping the neon green fanny pack in the nearest garbage can he could find.

They spent that afternoon and the next at the basketball court, playing pick-up games with Alejandro's friends. There wasn't any riding the pine for Nate, either. He played alongside Rachel and Alejandro both times and actually fared pretty well. Even when he did flub a shot or miss a pass, his teammates would shrug it off. "*La próxima vez*," they'd say. "Next time."

On the second day, as they walked out of a market where they'd bought bottles of ice-cold Coca-Cola, Alejandro said, "Tonight is Opening Ceremony. We can watch on television."

And so, after another gut-busting Spanish meal made by Señorita Vargas, the three teens hunkered down in front of the blocky television in the living room and watched the ceremony. The programming was in Spanish, so Nate was not certain exactly what was said, but the ceremony's colorful action captivated him.

When the American team was introduced, and the Dream Team walked along in blue blazers and white hats, Alejandro was more excited than Nate and Rachel. "There! Michael Jordan! Magic Johnson! I cannot believe it! They are all here!"

Nate didn't have the heart to tell his new friend what he and Rachel had seen in Monte

Carlo, or that two tickets to the gold-medal game were in his backpack.

The ceremony ended with a man in a white shirt and shorts carrying the Olympic torch through the stadium by spotlight. He passed it to another who ran to a platform and held the torch aloft as a man carrying a bow and arrow stepped forward.

"No way," Nate said as the torchbearer lit the end of the archer's arrow.

The bowman turned, aimed, and released the flaming arrow.

It arced through the sky, landing in a giant metal cauldron. The cauldron burst into flames as the crowd roared its approval.

"Cool," Rachel said in awe.

Alejandro leapt to his feet. He rushed to the living room window and threw it open. A warm breeze slipped through the room. "Come!" he shouted. "Look!"

Nate and Rachel joined him at the window. They could hear the roar of the far away crowd.

And there, in the distance, just a flicker of light on the horizon, was the enormous fire created by the Olympic torch.

CHAPTER 7

The days bled one into the next.

Nate and Rachel spent their time with Alejandro and his friends. When they weren't shooting hoops at the schoolyard, they were playing video games at Alejandro's on his Nintendo system.

"Whoa," Nate said when he saw the NES. "Old school."

"What do you mean?" Alejandro looked confused.

Nate waved him off. "Nothing."

The trio of teens also watched a number of Olympic events in the Vargas' living room. They watched U.S sprinter Gail Devers win gold in the 100-meter dash. And Chinese diver Fu Mingxia win gold at the age of thirteen, the youngest athlete to ever win top prize.

Their main focus, though, was definitely the Dream Team. They excitedly watched the United States demolish Angola in their first game by a score of 116-48. The following day, the United States played the country of Croatia. One of the Croatian players, an all-star named Tony Kukoc, was defended heavily by both Michael Jordan and Scottie Pippen.

"Kukoc will be playing for Bulls in NBA," Alejandro explained to them, translating the announcers' play-by-play. "They are giving him a taste of what to expect."

Kukoc and the Croatians couldn't stop the Dream Team. The United States won, 103-70.

And so it went, each day another win for Team U.S.A. What had happened in that closed gym in Monte Carlo had affected the way they played. They beat every opponent by no less than thirty points.

One day, Nate, Rachel, and Alejandro rode the tram to the Palau Municipal d'Esports de Badalona, where the basketball tournament was held. Throngs of people stood outside, waiting to catch a glimpse of the American all-stars.

As they passed a street vendor selling hot dogs, Nate spied a familiar face.

"Hey!" Harry Underhill had seen them, as well. He was waving his tamale in the air. "You're the kids from the train station."

"Hi," Nate said.

Harry took a bite of his food and made a face like it was pure poison. He wiped his chin with a napkin. "Terrible. Sorry. I've been hurrying around like crazy, trying to catch an interview with Coach Daly. I haven't had a chance to taste any good local flavor."

"You should have dinner with us." Nate made the offer before even thinking about it.

Harry looked confused. "What do you mean, kid?"

"My mother is an excellent cook," Alejandro explained. "The finest in Barcelona."

"Well, that's a bold claim." He thought about it a moment. "But I could sure use a bit of authentic cooking. Deal." He dumped the rest of his tamale in the trash.

Alejandro gave him the address, which Harry jotted down in a small notepad he kept in his suit coat's breast pocket.

"If I can track down Daly," he said, "I'll be there tonight."

Sure enough, as the teens set the table that evening and Señorita Vargas put the finishing touches on a bubbling pot of paella, the small buzzer by the apartment door sounded.

Alejandro pressed the intercom. "*Quién es?*" he asked. "Who is it?"

"Uh, Harry Underhill," the tinny voice in the speaker replied.

Harry arrived with a handful of wildflowers. When he saw Señorita Vargas, his eyes grew wide. "Good evening, ma'am," he said, removing his hat. "For you." He handed her the flowers.

"*Gracias*," she said.

They sat around the table, enjoying the delicious paella. Harry regaled them with stories from his days as a journalist, covering the NBA and the NFL and every Olympic Games since he first became a sportswriter. He even brought up a certain colleague of his, "A buddy of mine named Sam Winstead."

Nate, who'd just taken a bite of food, nearly shot rice out of his nostrils at the mention of Grandpa Sam.

When they'd finished eating, and Alejandro had run out of questions to ask about his favorite basketball players, Harry said, "Well, this has been an absolutely wonderful evening. I hate to leave, but I've got a deadline to hit." He stood and turned to Señorita Vargas. "Thank you so much for your hospitality, Carmen."

She held up one finger. "You cannot forget dessert." She rushed into the kitchen, coming back out a moment later with a paper bag. "Churros Con Chocolate," she said.

Harry's eyebrows rose. "Fried dough, cinnamon, and chocolate," he said, "Finally. A woman after my heart."

Señorita Vargas laughed and handed him the paper bag.

With an extra spring in his step and a hum on his lips, Harry bid them goodbye and whisked out the apartment door.

The morning of the gold medal game, Nate woke early. It was partly because Rachel had been snoring, but also because he was excited. Finally, after watching all of the games on television, he was going to see one in person. Sure, he knew the outcome already, but the thrill of experiencing history firsthand never wavered.

It was so early that even Señorita Vargas was still asleep. Nate snuck down to the small cafe near the apartment building and used the rest of his money to buy as many pastries as he could.

Alejandro was awake when he returned. "I'm so excited," he said. "Today is the gold-medal game. A rematch between the Dream Team and Croatia."

Nate nodded. For over a week, he'd listened to his new friend talk about the Dream Team like they were Greek gods. And really, they kind of were. In Nate's time, the NBA wasn't as popular as it was in the 1990s. Sure, there were all-stars who made the game look easy. But there wouldn't be players like Magic Johnson, Larry Bird, and Michael Jordan ever again. These guys not only played great basketball, they made basketball the greatest game in the world.

Nate had seen these athletic giants play. So he understood Alejandro's excitement.

But watching it on TV?

Nate thought of the tickets in his bag, and how hard it was going to be to tell Alejandro that he and Rachel were going to the game. And that was when he realized he didn't *have* to tell Alejandro, that he didn't have to break bad news to his new friend.

So when Rachel and Señorita Vargas joined he and Alejandro for breakfast, he just came out and said it. Without consulting Rachel. Without overthinking it.

He took the tickets from his bag and placed them on the table.

"These are for you guys," he said. "For your gracious hospitality."

For a minute, no one said a thing. Nate didn't want to look at Rachel, for fear that she was staring daggers at him. He couldn't help it, though. He glanced over.

She was smiling.

"What is this?" Alejandro inspected the tickets on the table.

"They're tickets to today's gold medal game," Nate said.

"For us?"

"For you and your mom. Go see the Dream Team wi—*play* for the gold."

"These are real?"

Nate laughed. "They're real."

Alejandro was beside himself. "I get to see the Dream Team! *I get to see the Dream Team.*" He followed by shouting a number of things in

Spanish, things that Nate didn't understand but that made his smiling mother wince and cover her ears.

The four of them took the tram back down to the arena. Alejandro couldn't sit still. He bounced with energy, proudly wearing the Charles Barkley T-shirt he'd been wearing the day Nate and Rachel met him.

As they approached the crowd outside the arena, Nate saw Harry Underhill leaning against a palm tree. "Well, who do we have here?" the journalist asked.

Nate opened his mouth to explain, but before he could, Alejandro blurted out, "I get to see the Dream Team!"

Harry laughed as Señorita Vargas held up the two tickets.

"I'll be," he said. "Looks like I'm not going to this game alone after all."

Alejandro turned to Nate and Rachel. "We will see you after game?" he asked.

Nate didn't think so. He shook his head. "We've got to head back," he said.

Alejandro lunged forward and wrapped Nate up in a big hug. "*Gracias*," he said.

"Have fun, dude," Nate said.

They said their goodbyes, and Nate and Rachel watched as Harry Underhill led Alejandro and his mom toward the arena. Soon, they were lost in the shuffle of fans, gone.

And that was when Nate felt the spark.

Of course, he thought with a smile.

"It's time, isn't it?" Rachel sensed it before he'd even said anything.

"Yep."

The two teens made their way through the crowd. They ducked behind a palm tree, out of sight. Nate pulled the *Sports Illustrated* out of his bag. It crackled with blue energy.

"It's been a blast," Rachel said.

Nate looked over at the arena just as a mighty roar of cheers filled the air. "*Adios*, Barcelona," he said.

Nate flipped open the magazine as tendrils of energy enveloped his hand.

Three brilliant flashes of light erupted from the magazine, and, in an instant, everything went black.

CHAPTER 8

Coming home was the best part.

Nate loved the adventure; he loved the sights and sounds, the thrill of seeing history made right before his eyes. But more than anything, he loved coming home.

He knew he was home before the world came into focus. He lay on the ground, his hands pressed against the cold cement of Grandpa Sam's driveway. He could feel the weight of his winter coat, the stocking cap on his head. The first breath he drew felt like needles in his lungs.

He was beyond the sunny skies of Monte Carlo and Barcelona. He was cold again. But Nate didn't care.

I'm home.

Nate staggered to his feet. Rachel was beside him.

"You okay?" he asked.

She nodded, wiping snow and grit from her bare palms. "Would have been nice to jump back and be in my nice warm bedroom," she said.

That wasn't how it worked, though. Because even after spending what amounted to two weeks in 1992, barely any time had elapsed for Nate and Rachel in the present.

Hence, the driveway.

Hence, the cold.

The issue of *Sports Illustrated* lay on the cement. Nate picked it up and brushed it off. He'd have to sneak it back down to Grandpa Sam's basement.

The two teens made their way back into the warmth of the cabin.

They shed their coats inside the door, and Nate slid the rolled magazine into the waistband of his pants. He covered it with his shirt just as his dad called out, "Hey, you two! Come say goodbye to the Underhills!"

The Underhills?

Nate and Rachel exchanged a puzzled look before hurrying into the kitchen to figure out what was going on.

Nate's heart tripped and thudded against his ribcage when he saw Harry Underhill seated in the kitchen with his arm around none other than Señorita Vargas. Alejandro's mom was as beautiful as Nate had remembered. Her salt and pepper hair had more gray in it now, and the lines around her kind eyes had deepened, but she was still the same woman who'd opened her home to them in Barcelona.

I can't believe that was only minutes ago for us, but over two decades for her.

Señorita Vargas smiled. "Oh, *dios mi*," she said. "It still amazes me how much you two have grown."

Nate couldn't believe it. Harry and Señorita Vargas had fallen in love and gotten married. The thought that he and Rachel were partially responsible for that made him grin from ear to ear.

Harry stood. He helped Señorita Vargas to her feet. "Well, we best be going," he said. "Still have to pack."

"When's your flight leave?" Grandpa Sam asked.

"Tomorrow afternoon."

"I'm so jealous," Rachel's mom said. "I'd love to see Spain someday."

"It's beautiful," Rachel blurted out.

Her mom looked at her quizzically. "Oh really? And when were you there?"

"Oh . . . I mean, I've seen tons of photos," Rachel said, recovering nicely. "Duh. The Internet, Mom."

Harry and Señorita Vargas gave a round of hugs. When Nate hugged Señorita Vargas, a wave of familiarity washed over him.

"Please make sure to give Alejandro our best," Nate's dad said.

Alejandro! The boy they'd played basketball with in Barcelona was now at least thirty years old.

"And congratulations on becoming grandparents," Nate's mom added.

"*Gracias*," Señorita Vargas said. "Alejandro and his wife are so blessed."

"Grandpa Harry?" Harry winced as the words rolled around on his tongue. "I'm too young to be a grandpa. Now you on the other hand . . . . " He playfully poked Grandpa Sam in the stomach.

After the Underhills left, the rest of the family cleaned up, and Nate covertly found his way back down into the basement. He left the lights off, opting instead to sneak over to the shelf on the wall in the dark. Faint blue moonglow lit his way.

He removed the *Sports Illustrated*, gave it one last press, and placed it back on the shelf. He wished he could replace the ticket stubs, as well, but they had been lost in the shuffle of time. He just hoped that Grandpa Sam would never notice their absence.

With one last glance at the smiling quintet of Hall of Fame athletes on the magazine's cover, Nate made his way back upstairs without anyone knowing he'd been absent.

Nate always assumed that after a long, tiring adventure, he'd be able to curl up in his warm, safe bed and sleep like a hibernating bear. But it never happened, and that night was no exception. He was too amped up to sleep.

So he found himself wide awake at three in the morning, lying on his back in bed, flipping a basketball into the air above him and catching it. Flipping it. Catching it.

He kept thinking of the Dream Team. Of watching The Greatest Game That Nobody Ever Saw, and playing pick-up ball with Alejandro and his friends.

But now that he was back in his own time, his focus shifted from the past to the future. More specifically, to the basketball game the Warriors had against the Eagleton Cyclones.

The last time Nate had seen his teammates, they'd been fighting in the locker room. They were stretching the meaning of the word *team*.

Before they'd jumped through time (which felt like a lifetime ago), Harry Underhill had told Nate the Warriors needed their own version of The Greatest Game in Monte Carlo.

"He's right," Nate said, flipping the ball one last time and catching it.

So the following morning, after sleep had finally found him and he woke to a crisp new winter day, Nate grabbed his phone off the nightstand and sent out a mass text message.

CHAPTER 9

"This better be good, Winstead," Jaden Kershaw said. "It's freezing out here."

"Yeah," Vic Gonzalez added, "I was still in bed watching SportsCenter." He tugged his blue and yellow Warriors stocking cap low on his ears.

Nate stood under the hoop at the concrete court in Wells Municipal Park. To his surprise, most of the team had actually responded to Nate's text; they were huddled around him now, jumping up and down or blowing into their gloves. Nate had a basketball tucked under one arm. Rachel stood beside him, looking tougher than any of the wimps trying to stay warm around her.

"Guys," Nate started. "At the end of our last game, we fell apart. We looked like a bunch of glory-seekers, and not a team. And if we keep that up, we're gonna get our butts kicked by Eagleton."

"We'll only lose if I'm not the one taking the shots," Jaden boasted.

"Nah," Vic countered. "I hate to break it to you, but letting you shoot is how we get beat, Kershaw."

"I don't see you making clutch shots."

"Because you don't give me a chance."

Nate spoke up. "Well, now's your chance," he said. "Full-on scrimmage. No refs. No Coach Webster."

"And we're gonna do it out here?" Paolo asked.

"Look around," Rachel said, nodding at the park. Aside from a couple of young kids being pulled in sleds by their parents, the place was empty. "No one's watching."

A wide smile spread across Jaden's face. "Let's do this."

"Jaden and Vic, you're captains," Nate said, feeling like Chuck Daly commanding his troops. "Pick your teams."

The Warriors split in two, with Nate picked by Jaden—his last choice, of course—and Rachel

scooped up by Vic—not his last choice. Of course.
As Paolo and Breckin Morris lined up for the tip-off,
Nate said, "All ya got now, fellas. All ya got."

He tossed the ball high into the air. The two
centers leaped up for it, and Paolo tipped it back into
Jaden's hands.

Like Jordan and Johnson facing off, Jaden
dribbled the ball toward the hoop with Vic guarding
him. The two started taunting each other right
away. "You think you can play defense on me?"
Jaden asked. He broke left, dribbled behind his back,
then came back to the right.

Vic cut him off. "You know it," he said, smirking.

Jaden pulled up. Vic was right there, and he
batted Jaden's jumper away. The ball went rolling.
Vic didn't even have to say anything as Jaden felt
the sting of the rejection for the entire time it took
one of the other guys to retrieve the ball.

"Check ball," said Jaden, when the ball was
finally returned to his hands. He bounced it to Vic,
who bounced it back.

Jaden began to dribble, working back and forth. Again he made a charge and looked to pull up. Instead of shooting, though, he gave a head fake. Vic bit, and Jaden dished the ball to Paolo under the hoop. Paolo put up an easy bank shot that rattled the backboard and slid through the chain hoop.

"Count it!" Paolo shouted.

"Boom!" Jaden said right in Vic's face. "Let's see what you got now!"

The game continued like that, players jawing at each other, throwing elbows and joking around. At first, the rhythm was off, and the game play was slow. But as they warmed up, and the biting cold weather was temporarily forgotten, they fell into a comfortable pattern of play.

Nate even got in on the trash-talking after he and Jaden performed a perfect give-and-go. Nate turned to Rachel, who'd been defending him, and said, "Boo-yah! In your face!"

Rachel, expressionless, shook her head. "Just . . . just don't."

Once, as Andy Hewitt drove through the lane, he passed behind his back to Paolo, who leapt so high, his fingers brushed the rim as he sunk the lay-up.

"Whoa!" Vic said. "Nice move!"

"I call it the 'Sneak Attack,'" Andy said.

By the time the last jump shot had been sunk, Jaden's team had come out ahead. *But what matters more*, thought Nate, *is that the Warriors are having fun and getting along.*

Nate hoped that the feeling would hang around.

CHAPTER 10

Nate and Rachel stood just outside the gymnasium at Wells Middle School. Rachel stared blank-faced at Nate. He was wearing his blue and yellow basketball uniform. He had his fists on his hips, trying out his best superhero pose.

"Well?" Nate asked. "Whaddaya think?"

Rachel shrugged. "What do I think of what? I've seen your basketball uniform before, dude."

"Not that." He tapped his toes and shuffled his feet. "You're missing the best part."

Rachel got the hint. She looked down and said, "Whoa. Are those . . . ?"

"My dad's old Air Jordans. Pretty sweet, huh?"

Nate's dad had searched through his old boxes in the basement to find the sneakers. When he finally located them, he handed them over with pride to his son.

The black and red hightop sneakers were a little big for Nate, but he didn't mind. "I'm wearing them for good luck," he said, smiling.

"You're gonna need it," she said. She gave him a playful shove. "Now go out there and warm that bench, Winstead."

Nate rolled his eyes. "Thanks a lot," he said.

The crowd was much larger than usual for a middle school basketball game. The bleachers were full. Some fans were forced to stand along the wall, their winter coats draped over one arm. The town of Eagleton was near Wells, and it seemed like their entire population had traveled to watch their undefeated squad face off against the Warriors.

Coach Webster paced courtside, chomping away on a wad of gum, watching his Warriors warm up. As Nate nervously made his way to the bench, Vic Gonzalez passed him and said, "Killer kicks, bro."

The large Air Jordans nearly did him in during warm-ups. As Nate broke to the hoop, he tripped over his own feet and had to chuck the ball up toward the hoop. Thankfully, his shot banked off the board and in. "Planned that," he said under his breath.

The massive crowd quieted to a dull rumble as each team's starting five jogged onto the court. Nate took his usual spot by the water bottles, hoping that whatever had been broken after their last loss, the Warriors' outdoor scrimmage had mended it.

Paolo faced off against the Cyclones' center, who was so tall he looked like he belonged on the varsity team. He sneered down at Paolo.

The ref blew the whistle and tossed the ball up. The Cyclone center swatted it into the waiting hands of their point guard, a short but quick kid who moved like a waterbug. he brought the ball up the court, shouting numbers at his offense. Jaden stuck to him like Coach Webster's wad of bubble gum, crouching low and following the speedster's every step.

The Cyclones' shooting guard set a pick on Jaden, and before Andy Hewitt could pick up Jaden's man on defense, the point guard had dished the ball inside to the hulking center, who flipped it up and in.

This isn't gonna be pretty, Nate thought.

Jaden brought the ball up the court for the Warriors, and it was like they picked up right where they left off after their last game. He took a couple of directionless dribbles and, instead of passing the ball, jacked up a clunker of a jump shot.

The Cyclones' center effortlessly boarded the miss and chucked the ball to mid-court where their guard was already on a fast break. One easy lay-up later, the Warriors were down by four.

Coach Webster's gum took the brunt of his anger. He chewed it so viciously, Nate was surprised the man's jaw didn't snap.

The next time down the court, Vic Gonzalez wove through the lane and tried a fancy maneuver through double-coverage. The ball bounced off his foot and rolled out of bounds. Another Warriors turnover.

Nate could hardly sit. He wanted to jump up in frustration, pace around like Coach Webster. He tapped his Air Jordans loudly on the wood floor. "Come on, Warriors!" he shouted.

The first half of the game was brutal. The Warriors were able to put some points up on the board, but the Cyclones had them figured out. They doubled-up whoever had the ball because the likelihood of a pass was slim.

Nate was able to get out onto the court for a few minutes near the end of the half. As he jogged over to sub in, Rachel called out, "Be like Mike!"

Nate tried not to smile. He failed.

His one-size-too-large high tops made it feel like he was playing in clown shoes. Nate didn't care, though. When a rebound came his way, he put up a smooth jump hook that banked in off the glass.

"Way to go, Nate!" his dad bellowed.

All that practice in Barcelona is paying off, Nate thought.

The Cyclones, led by their massive center and speedster point guard, had an impressive offense. Whenever the ball came the center's way, he gobbled it up. There was no catching them, not the way the Warriors were playing.

At the end of the first half, Nate and the Wells Warriors were down 45-30.

In the locker room at halftime, Coach Webster spit his gum into a trashcan. It tinked against the metal receptacle. "What's going on out there, guys?" he growled.

Jaden slammed his fist into a locker, but no one said a thing.

"How many times have I told you to take smart shots? Use your heads. There's five of you on the court. For crying out loud, trust each other!"

The Warriors received the ball at the start of the second half. Andy passed the ball inbounds to Jaden, who dribbled it up the court. The Cyclones doubled him up, leaving Paolo undefended under the hoop.

"Pass!" Paolo shouted.

Instead, Jaden tried to dribble through the defense. The ball was stripped away and two Cyclones took off on a fast break. As one went for a lay-up, Jaden was able to hustle back and knock the ball free.

Andy Hewitt scooped it up and broke down the court. He was flanked by Paolo, whose long strides carried him quickly to the hoop. The massive Cyclones center stood in Andy's way. Andy eyed up the hoop, not even looking at Paolo. Nate popped out of his chair, cupped his hands around his mouth, and shouted, "Sneak attack!"

Andy's ears perked up. He'd heard Nate. As the center lunged forward, Andy looped the ball behind his back, past the defender, and right into the hands of Paolo, who laid it in.

"Yes!" Nate shouted. He and a bench buddy bumped fists.

The tide shifted, and the next time down the court, Jaden found Vic in the corner for a long three-pointer. The Warriors bench—and its fans— jumped to their feet.

"Count it!" Vic shouted as he and Jaden slapped five.

"Back on D!" Coach Webster continued to pace the sideline.

The lead was down to ten. Nate watched as his team hit shot after shot. Paolo with an easy lay-up in the paint. Andy dishing to Jaden on a give-and-go for a jump shot. A fast break that ended with a Vic Gonzalez lay-up. The Cyclones' center was a tough person to stop, though. Jump hook left. Spin move right. Fadeaway. Up and under. He singlehandedly kept his team in the lead.

With less than a minute remaining, Kendrick went for one last fake from the Cyclones' man in the middle and fouled out.

"Winstead!"

Nate leapt to his feet as the coach called his name. Coach Webster said, "I need somebody out there to put a body on their big man. Be physical. If you have to foul, so be it. Let's make him beat us from the line. Got it?"

Nate nodded. "Sure thing, Coach." He checked into the game for Kendrick and glanced up at the clock. Just 48 seconds left, and they were down by four points.

The Cyclones' center hit the first free throw but missed the second. The ball was up for grabs, and it glanced off Nate's hands before a Cyclones player snatched it. Nate shook his head and crouched low, determined to play tough defense on the center. Out of the corner of his eye, he saw the point guard scoot past the defense and shovel a pass in his direction.

Nate spun, swatted at the ball, and knocked it off-track. He chased after it, narrowly beating the point guard. Paolo rocketed up the center of the court. Nate saw him, and heaved the ball over his head. Paolo plucked it out of the air, dribbled twice, and laid the ball up and in.

Just 23 seconds left. *Down by three!*

The Cyclones plan was to run out the clock. The point guard dribbled into trouble and threw it high where only the tall center could reach. The center held the ball over everyone's head like some big brother. Nate looked over at the bench.

"Do it, Winstead!" Coach shouted.

Nate jumped high and slapped at the ball, hitting the center's hand.

Tweep! The ref pointed at Nate. "Foul!"

The Wells side of the bleachers began to stomp its feet as the Cyclones' center lined up at the free throw line for a one-and-one. The noise coming from the Wells fans sounded like a thunderstorm that had erupted inside the gym. The thunderstorm shook the Cyclone center, whose foul shot hit side rim.

"Go!" yelled Coach Webster. "Go!" He waved them down the court.

Paolo dished ahead to Nate, who found Jaden at the top of the key. Jaden put up a three-pointer.

Swish! Tie game!

With just 16 ticks left on the clock, the Cyclones were back on their heels. They called timeout to get their bearings.

The Warriors huddled around Coach Webster. He said, "They're gonna get it to their big guy. Try for the steal but foul him if you need to." He looked directly at Nate when he said it. Nate nodded.

"And when we get the ball back," Coach Webster said, "remember to only take—"

The whole team finished for him, saying, "*Smart shots!*"

The Cyclones lined up for the inbound pass. The Cyclone guards split apart, dancing around the court. Nate spied the Cyclone inbounder staring down the center. Nate broke for the center, his Air Jordans squeaking with each step, as the inbounder threw a two-handed over-the-head pass. Nate jumped into the air, reached out, and tipped the ball away before the center could catch it.

The ball landed right in Vic Gonzalez's hands!

"Smart shots!" Coach Webster shouted. "Smart shots!"

Vic hurried the ball up the court as the Cyclone defense put on the full-court press. At mid-court, Vic whipped the ball over to Jaden.

Nine seconds left!

Jaden sized up the defender. It looked like he was going to drive to the hoop. He dribbled forward, pulled up, and gave a head fake. The defender bit, skying high for the block. Jaden skipped the ball down to Paolo where Cyclones quickly swarmed him in the paint.

Five seconds . . . four seconds . . .

Without looking, Paolo bounce-passed back, right into the hands of Nate, who was wide open.

Three seconds . . . two seconds!

Nate eyed up the hoop, pretending that he was back on a concrete court in Barcelona with Rachel and Alejandro, playing a breezy pick-up game.

Nate exhaled, jumped into the air, and released the ball. It sailed in a high arc. The whole gym watched as the ball hit front iron, glanced off the backboard, rattled the rim again . . .

. . . and dropped in.

The buzzer blared through the gym.

The Warriors swarmed the court, rushing over to Nate. Paolo picked him up in a bone-crushing bear hug. Jaden gave him a happy shove and said, "Nice jumper, Winstead."

Nate looked over and saw Rachel running
onto the court. Behind her, in the stands, were his
parents, his aunt, and Grandpa Sam.

Rachel gave him a slap on the shoulder, laughed,
and said, "It's gotta be the shoes."

ABOUT THE AUTHOR

Brandon Terrell is the author of numerous children's books, including several volumes in both the Tony Hawk 900 Revolutions series and the Tony Hawk Live2Skate series. He has also written the first four titles from the Sports Illustrated Kids Time Machine Magazine set and the latest titles in the Jim Nasium series. When not hunched over his laptop, Brandon enjoys watching movies and television, reading, watching (and playing!) baseball, and spending time with his wife and two children in Minnesota.

ABOUT THE ILLUSTRATOR

Passionate comic book fan and artist Eduardo Garcia works from his studio in Mexico City. Since signing with Space Goat Productions in 2012, he has brought his talent, pencils, and ink to such varied projects as Spider-Man Family (Marvel), Flash Gordon (Ardden), and Speed Racer (IDW).

GLOSSARY

center – position involving playing near the basket; usually filled by tallest players; also called "five" or "post"

drive – an offensive move in which a player dribbles the ball toward the hoop in order to shoot from closer up

fast break – play or method that involves the offensive team advancing the ball from one end of the court to the other very quickly by way of fast dribbling or passing

forward – position involving playing both outside and inside; also called "three," "four," "small forward," "power forward," or "wing"

give-and-go – two-man basketball play where player A passes to player B and then breaks to the hoop, receiving a pass back from player B

pick-and-roll – two-man basketball play where Player A sets a pick and then rolls to the basket as Player B either dribble drives to the hoop for a shot or passes back to Player A

point guard – position in basketball involving dribbling, passing, shooting, and directing the team on offense; usually filled by smallest, quickest players; also called "one" or "point"

putback – in basketball, the act of getting a rebound and quickly shooting it back into the hoop

shooting guard – position in basketball involving shooting, scoring, and ballhandling on offense; also called "two" or "off-guard"

TIMELESS FACTS: DREAM TEAM

▶ Marked the first collection of professional players to participate in United States Olympic basketball.

▶ Captained by by Magic Johnson, who came out of retirement to play in Barcelona after previously retiring due to HIV diagnosis following the 1990–91 NBA season.

▶ Won all eight of their Olympic contests by an average of 44 points per game.

▶ Captured the gold medal with a 117-85 win over Croatia.

▶ Led by Charles Barkley in scoring (18 points per game), Karl Malone and Chris Mullin in rebounding (5.3 per game), Scottie Pippen in assists (7.8 per game), Michael Jordan in steals (4.6 per game), Patrick Ewing in blocks (1.9 per game), and Christian Laettner in free throw shooting (90 percent).

▶ Inducted into the National Basketball Hall of Fame in 2010.

TIMELESS FACTS:
THE 1992 BARCELONA OLYMPICS

▶ Was the first Games since 1972 that didn't involve boycotts.

▶ Was also the first Olympics since the fall of the communist governments in Eastern Europe.

▶ West and East Germany entered together as one country for the first time since the Berlin Wall was built.

▶ For the first time since 1936, Latvia, Lithuania, and Estonia entered independently. Other former Soviet Union countries competed together as "the Unified Team."

▶ First appearance for South Africa, newly free from apartheid, after a 32-year ban.

▶ Was the first time Namibia competed in the Olympic Games. The country used to be under South Africa's rule.

▶ Was the last time the Winter and Summer Games would be held in the same year.

▶ Spain spent 8 billion dollars to prepare Barcelona to host the Games.

▶ Competitions held in badminton, baseball, and women's judo for the first time.

FIND YOUR MOMENT IN TIME WITH

SPORTS ILLUSTRATED KIDS

TIME MACHINE MAGAZINE

TIME MACHINE MAGAZINE

DATE DUE

Demco